# Dear Girl You are Amazing

### Inspiring stories about courage, inner strength, and confidence

## Emily Green

# Content

# Introduction

Hey there! Do you know that you are very special? There are millions of girls in this world. But there is only one of you. You are completely unique. Always remember that!

The world has many big and small hurdles in store for you. Sometimes you might think that you can't make it. You might get very scared or doubt yourself. However, I want to tell you a secret. Everybody feels like this from time to time! Even adults. Life without hurdles and problems does not exist. Where there is good, there is also bad.

Even things that scare you or you would prefer not to do are a part of your life. Sometimes, bad experiences can also reveal something good.

You will meet many girls in the stories of this book. Girls who didn't dare at first but then courageously conquered their fears. Girls who doubted themselves but then showed inner strength. Girls who almost gave up but then discovered their confidence and didn't give up.
I am sure that you can do all of this too. But you must start believing in yourself. These stories will help you with that.

You will find a picture with an important message after each story. Feel free to color the picture. It's best to use lots of bright colors. This way, you will better remember the messages and never forget them, even in the difficult moments of your life. Remember that you are unique, lovable, and important to this world.

You are wonderful just the way you are!

# I AM
# SPECIAL

# The first day of school

Mary was nervous. She barely slept last night. At breakfast this morning, she only got a few bites down, but it wasn't because of the food. The six-year-old girl usually loved her sandwiches with butter and raspberry jam. Today, she didn't like any of it. She couldn't even stand the hot cocoa that she typically happily drank each morning.

"Aren't you hungry, sweetheart?" asked Mary's mom with concern.
"Today is your special day, after all! You should eat plenty so that you are prepared for the day," she continued.

Her mom was right. Mary really did have an exciting day ahead of her. It was her first day of school.

On the one hand, she looked forward to it, and she hadn't been able to think about anything else for weeks. On the other hand, she was somewhat insecure and nervous. There was a reason for that.

Mary had just moved to another city with her parents. Her dad found a new job with another company. Mary was not thrilled about this at all. All her kindergarten friends were now far away from her. She didn't know anyone in this city yet. She desperately wished that she would finally make lots of new friends at school.

"Today, you finally have your first day of school.

You've been waiting for this day for so long, and now it's finally here! Aren't you excited?" asked her mom with a smile on her face.

Of course she noticed that Mary was very excited. That's why she tried to cheer up her daughter a little.

Mary replied, "Yes, I am happy. But I feel a little uneasy. I'm sure all the other children know each other from kindergarten. But I'm all alone here. What if no one wants to talk to me or sit next to me?"

Mary lowered her head, and a small tear rolled down her left cheek.

She was always open and honest with her

mom because she knew she could talk to her about anything. Her mom walked up to her and hugged her tightly, lovingly stroking the back of her head.

"Don't worry, my sweetheart," her mom said in a gentle voice. "Why wouldn't you make new friends? You are such a nice and friendly girl. If I had to go to school again, I would want to sit next to you right away," her mom said with positivity

Her words calmed Mary down a little again. "Mom is almost always right," the little girl thought hopefully.

Mary was now full of newfound courage. She ran out into the hallway. There, she put on her new pink sandals with little glittering stones that she received as a gift from her grandma. She then slipped into her favorite pink jacket. Next, she picked up her satchel. Its color was also pink, and it had her favorite animal, a horse, printed on the front.

"Are you ready?" asked her mom. Mary just nodded. "Let's go, then!" Mary joined her mom in the car, and they headed off to school.

During the car ride, her mom kept giving her little daughter an encouraging, joyful smile. Then she told her a story: "Oh, I still remember my first day of school. I was so excited at the time and didn't really want to go to school. But then I learned to read, do math, and write. I made so many new friends. Someday, I'm sure you'll be grateful that you were able to go to school."

Mary listened to her mom's words, and somehow, she could hardly wait to be there now.

Her mom stopped the car, and the engine fell silent. They had arrived at school. Mary saw the big blue building with brightly painted windows. She watched the many children and parents gathering around the entrance. Some children stood together in groups where they talked and giggled. Mary thought to herself that these children must have been in the second or even third grade. She watched the crowd with wide eyes. Somehow, her nervousness came back. Mom lovingly took her hand, leaned over, and whispered in her ear, "Come on, we're going to look for your classroom together now. It's surely the most beautiful one in the whole school!"

Everything looked so big and new, including the long hallways and the many colorful pictures on the walls. There were so many children who were somehow all having fun and chatting with each other. She was getting more and more excited to be a school kid, too, finally. Her classroom was in the right wing of the school. Mary's homeroom teacher, Miss Summers, was already happily waiting outside the door to greet everyone. She looked very nice, wearing a beautiful dress with a sweater

over it. Her brown hair
was pinned up in a bun.
Seeing Mary, she said
cheerfully:

"Welcome. It's good to
have you here. You can
pick out a seat you'd like
to sit in right now."

In her excitement, Mary
could only bring a shy,
"Okay," to her lips.

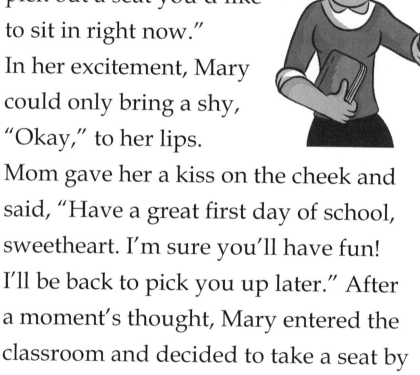

Mom gave her a kiss on the cheek and
said, "Have a great first day of school,
sweetheart. I'm sure you'll have fun!
I'll be back to pick you up later." After
a moment's thought, Mary entered the
classroom and decided to take a seat by
the window in the second row.

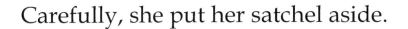

Carefully, she put her satchel aside.

She sat down and let her eyes wander
around the classroom for a moment.
The whiteboard already read "Welcome"
in large letters. Pictures with large letters
and numbers hung on the walls. Mary
watched the other children come in one by
one.

"Class 1A, please enter now," Miss
Summers called out to the children who
were still standing outside in the hallway
with their parents. A swarm of children
came into the classroom, not one of whom
Mary knew.

Her heart started pounding fast again
with excitement. She would have loved to
be back in preschool with her old friends

right now.

"Hey, is the seat next to you still free?" asked a girl in a light blue dress with long blonde curls.

"Yes, there's no one sitting there yet," Mary answered shyly.

The girl sat down next to Mary and introduced herself with a smile on her face, "I'm Anna."

"And my name is Mary," she quickly gushed. The two briefly smiled at each other and then began chatting about their time in preschool and their hobbies.

Mary and Anna hit it off right away and quickly realized that they had many things in common. For example, they both loved to draw pictures and play with dolls. In addition, horses were also Anna's favorite animals. Mary's worries about not making friends suddenly vanished. With Anna as her seatmate, she already felt much more comfortable. Who knows, maybe Anna would even become her best friend one day?

Mary could hardly wait to meet the other children in her class. Earlier, Mary would have liked to sink into a hole in the ground to hide. But now she was sure that she would make many new friends here and that she would enjoy school.

# I AM
# WONDERFUL

# The poem

"Jack and Jill
Went up the hill
To fetch a pail of water,
Jack fell down
And broke his crown
And Jill came tumbling after.
Up Jack got
And home did trot
As fast as he could caper,
Went to bed
To mend his head
With vinegar and brown paper."

Mel had finally done it. Now she knew all the lines of the poem by heart. Tomorrow she was supposed to recite the poem in front of the whole class. Mel was a second grader and eight years old. She had light brown shoulder-length hair and hazel eyes. Most days, she wore two braids. Mel had a great mom who helped her learn the poem. She recited the poem to her mom over and over again. She almost never made a mistake. If she got stuck, all her mom had to do was tell her the next word, and everything came back to her. Mel was annoyed even when she made tiny mistakes while reciting the poem.

Noticing this, her mom told her, "Oh, Mel, don't take the little mistakes so much to heart. They happen to everyone. Nothing and no one in this world are perfect." Mel knew that her mother was right. But still, she didn't want to make even one mistake.

She tried so hard because she wanted to get a good grade. After all, English was her best subject, along with sports.

She got a B on her report card last year. Mel was very proud of that. And of course, her mother was also proud that her little daughter was so good with words. But Mom didn't really care if she got an A, B, or whatever grade on her report card.

For her, the main thing was that Mel did her best and was happy.

In the evening, her mom came into Mel's room and said to her, "It's almost 9:00. Time to go to bed. Otherwise, you won't get out of bed tomorrow! You want to have lots of energy for the day, right?" Mom knew, of course, that Mel was supposed to recite the poem in English class tomorrow. While Mel was lying in her bed, she quietly recited the poem several more times from beginning to end: "Jack and Jill went up the hill to fetch a pail of water ..."
At some point, she finally fell asleep, exhausted. The next day, Mel had breakfast with her mother. She poked

around a little in her cereal. It wasn't that she didn't like it. Instead, it was the excitement that took away her appetite that morning.

"What's the matter, sweetheart? Why are you so quiet?" inquired Mel's mom.

"Oh, it's nothing!" replied Mel as she looked down at the floor, slightly embarrassed. Mel wanted to keep her fear to herself at first. But Mom just knew her too well and naturally sensed that Mel was upset about the poem. Mom put her hand on Mel's shoulder and looked at her encouragingly.

Then she spoke in a soft voice, "Don't worry about the poem. You've been studying just fine."

Mel slowly raised her head. Of course, she

had studied, but that was not her point.

Mel said sadly, "Yes, I did.... But what if I forget something, and then the other kids laugh at me?"

Immediately Mom replied, "I can't imagine anyone in your class laughing at you. Let me let you in on a secret.

The other kids are at least as excited as you are." Mom gave Mel a kiss on the forehead and gave her a loving hug.

Then, Mel packed her stuff and went to school. In the first lesson, she had math class. Normally, she always listened attentively and paid close attention.

But today, she had a hard time concentrating. She was just too nervous and couldn't think of anything other than the poem. It was good that she had English class right away in the second lesson and could finally recite the poem.

"Ding-dong" rang the school bell for second period.
Mel's class teacher, Mr. Brown, said:
"Today, we are going to recite the poem. I hope you all practiced well. Which one of you wants to start?"
The whole classroom immediately became quiet. You could have heard a pin drop. After about ten seconds of silence, which felt more like ten minutes to Mel, Mr. Brown continued, "All right. If none of you want to go first, I'm going to pick someone now."

All the children began to avoid eye contact with Mr. Brown in a panic. Mel's heart began to pound faster and faster. There was no way she was going to be the first to present. In her mind, she said to herself, "Please, not me. Please, not me."

Finally, Mr. Brown spoke up, "Mel! Will you please come forward and recite the poem for us."

"What a bummer!" thought Mel to herself. She walked to the whiteboard with wobbly legs. The other children were visibly relieved not to have to recite the poem first. Now they all eagerly looked at Mel. She began to recite the poem. In the first lines, she was still very nervous, and you could hear a tremor in her voice. But little by little, her anxiety diminished.

But then a sudden halt!
How did it go on again?
Mel's heart raced, and
she raised her eyes
in despair. Now, of
course, everyone was
looking at her with wide
eyes. But no one laughed, just as her
mom had said they wouldn't. Mr. Brown
noticed that Mel could not remember the
rest of the poem on her own.
"And Jill came tumbling after...." said Mr.
Brown, hoping to jog Mel's memory.
"Up Jack got, and home did trot!" cried
Mel, who now remembered again.
She recited the poem to the end without
mistakes.

"You did very well, Mel! Thank you so much! You may sit down again!"

Slowly all the pressure fell off Mel, and she felt liberated. After the lesson, she asked Mr. Brown what grade she had received.
A "B!" Mel smiled and was happy.

How nervous she had been! And now she had finally made it, and no one laughed, although she faltered briefly.
Mel was very proud of herself for not letting her fear get her down. She was sure

to have an even easier time with the next poem. And who knows, maybe one day she would speak in front of a lot of people and give big speeches? She also learned that it's usually not so bad if you make a mistake.

Mel couldn't wait to tell her mom all about it.

# I TRUST MYSELF

# The cinnamon bun

Mia woke up to the first rays of sunshine that Saturday morning. It was November, and winter had finally arrived. It was cold outside, and snowflakes covered the usually green meadows and trees.

Mia turned six years old last month. She's in first grade now.

Mia is a shy little girl with long black braids and big brown eyes. She likes winter more than summer. She just loves to build snowmen and go sledding with her friends.

Mia jumped out of bed in a good mood. Still in her pajamas, she left her little room and ran to the kitchen, beaming with joy. There, she saw her mom preparing breakfast. Her mom put cups, plates, and silverware on the dining table. She also prepared a fruit tea, the smell of which slowly spread throughout the room. "Yummy, that smells delicious," Mia thought to herself. Mom was putting the jam on the table as Mia walked in.

Mia smiled briefly at her mom and greeted her as always with a friendly "Good morning, Mom" and a kiss on the cheek. "Good morning, my sweetheart!" her mother replied and then continued in a more serious tone, "We have a little problem. Unfortunately, when I went shopping yesterday, I forgot to get rolls and pretzels for us. Could you please go to

the bakery and get some?"

Mia replied in surprise, "But I've never been shopping by myself! Can't we go together? Like always?" Mom replied, "I'm afraid we can't. Your little sister Lea caught a cold and is now coughing terribly. She really wants me to stay with her and take care of her."

Mia understood her mom. She loved her little sister Lea more than anything. Lea was only two years old. That's why Mom really shouldn't leave her alone. Especially not when she was sick, too. "All right, then I'll go alone," Mia finally said. Mom was visibly relieved and happy to have Mia's help, "Thank you, Mia. Please

get four rolls and three pretzels. And
as a reward, you may also buy a
cinnamon bun.

You like them so much.
I've already put the
money for them in
the pocket of your
winter jacket. It's
very sweet of you to
help me." Mia then changed her clothes.
She took off her pajamas and got dressed
for the cold weather outside. She didn't
want to catch a cold like her little sister.
On the one hand, Mia was really looking
forward to the cinnamon bun. She loved
cinnamon buns, and they had always
been her favorite. On the other hand, she
suddenly felt full of doubt and fear.

After all, she was a shy little girl who had never been shopping alone.

What if she couldn't get a word out at all, and the other people in line had to wait impatiently behind her? What if she completely forgot what she was supposed to bring home in the first place because she was so excited?

Thousands of thoughts flashed through Mia's mind. But she really wanted to make her mom proud and be a good role model to her little sister Lea. That's why she decided to go anyway. "See you soon, Mom," Mia said as she zipped up her winter jacket and walked out of the warm house into the cold, snowy winter day, her heart pounding.

Fortunately, the way to the bakery was neither very long nor dangerous. The bakery was just across the street, and there was also a crosswalk leading to it.

Before Mia crossed the street at the crosswalk, she looked left and right to see if a car was coming. She learned that from her mom. "Better safe than sorry," she used to say.

So, to be completely sure, she looked left and right again. Still no car in sight.

Mia crossed the street at the crosswalk and stood in front of the small blue house that read "BAKERY" in glowing yellow letters." Mia closed her eyes briefly, took three deep breaths, and hesitantly opened the door.

As soon as she entered the store, a bell rang. The ringing signaled the clerk that a new customer had arrived. "Good morning," Mia said in a slightly trembling voice.

She learned from Mom that you should always greet other people nicely.

That's why she made every effort to do the same today. The clerk greeted back in a friendly manner and then continued to serve an older lady who entered the bakery before Mia.

"That wasn't so hard!", Mia thought to herself and began to wrap her right index finger around her long black hair. She always did that when she was very excited. She then let her eyes wander around the store. She saw many pretzels, rolls, and even small and large cakes. And, of course, there were the cinnamon buns she loved so much! After the older lady paid, it was finally Mia's turn. Immediately, she became very nervous again. Her little heart started pounding loud and fast. She couldn't remember the last time she had been so excited.

"Hello, what would you like to have, young lady?" the clerk asked in a friendly tone.

"Hello, I.. I.. I'd like three rolls and four pretzels, please!" said Mia in a shaky voice.

Only a few seconds later, she realized that she had mixed up the numbers. "Sorry, I just got mixed up. Four rolls and three pretzels, I mean!" Mia corrected herself, visibly tense. "Oh, that's not a problem at all. It happens to a lot of customers," the clerk replied understandingly and smiled kindly at her.

She must have noticed how excited Mia was. "And then I'd like this cinnamon bun," Mia said as she pointed her index finger at a large cinnamon bun with frosting.

"All right. That will be exactly eight dollars," said the saleswoman, who put everything in a paper bag. Mia put a five-dollar bill and three dollars on the small tray. "Keep the change," Mia said confidently because she was sure she hadn't miscounted.

"Thank you very much, and goodbye. Enjoy!" said the clerk.

Mia said goodbye, nodded her head slightly and left the store.

Suddenly, a feeling of uncontrollable joy

arose in her. She could not describe what she felt at that moment. She had just gone shopping alone for the first time in her life. Although she was very excited and even once afraid of it, Mia didn't let it get her down. She also realized that it wasn't so bad to slip up and say something wrong. Because that can happen to anyone. "Maybe I'm not so shy after all," she thought to herself. Happy and in a good mood, Mia walked back home.

Once home, Mia could no longer hide her smile: "I bought everything for us, Mom. And I really enjoyed it! If you don't mind, I'll go shopping by myself more often in the future." Mom was overjoyed and praised her daughter, "You did a great job!

I'm very proud of you, Mia."

By now, Mia, Lea, and Mom were really hungry. They couldn't wait to finally start breakfast. At the table, Lea, who was luckily feeling much better, asked, "Can I please have some of your cinnamon bun?"

"Of course, I'll be happy to share with you," Mia replied immediately and broke off a piece for her little sister.

The two sisters ate the cinnamon bun with excitement. Yum!

"Life can be so beautiful when you step out of your comfort zone," Mia thought to herself.

I AM UNIQUE AND
IMPORTANT TO
THIS WORLD

# The shuttlecock

"Ding dong," the doorbell rang loudly.
Immediately, Lilly ran with big steps
through the hallway and opened the
apartment door with anticipation.
"Hi, I'm glad you came," Lilly said to her
best friend Sarah, beaming with joy.
Lilly and Sarah were both eight years old
and met in elementary school. Since then,
they have been almost inseparable. Almost
every week, the two of them
meet to spend time together.
Together they always have
lots of fun and never get
bored. "My mom made
a cake for us. Would you

like to try it?" asked Lilly. Sarah answered, "Yes, I would love to. I love cake!" They ran into the kitchen and gleefully ate the raspberry chocolate cake that Lilly's mom always covered with a little cream.

After they ate enough, Lilly and Sarah went out into the garden to play badminton together. It was a beautiful warm summer day in July. The sun was shining, and there was hardly a cloud in the bright blue sky. The lawn in the garden was a vibrant green, and the flowers were shining in their most beautiful colors. Neither of them had ever played badminton before.

Lilly's mom had only recently bought the two colorful rackets and the white shuttlecock.

In the beginning, the two of them played the ball slowly. But as time went by, they learned to control the ball better and better.

They got faster and faster. The ball flew higher and higher back and forth between the two of them.

But then it happened!

Sarah didn't hit the ball quite right, and the shuttlecock took off in a high arc, flying over the fence and into the neighbor's property. The ball landed in the middle of the flowerbed, of all places! For a moment, Lilly and Sarah looked at each other in silence. Sarah had a look of shock on her face, and her cheeks blushed. She was embarrassed about having hit the ball into someone else's garden.

"Which one of us is going to get the ball now?" asked Sarah uncertainly. "Well, you, of course. You hit the ball last. So, you have to bring it back!" Lilly answered immediately.

"But the ball isn't mine. It's yours, isn't it? I think you have to go get it!" said Sarah angrily. Lilly didn't feel like arguing with her best friend and remembered her mom's old saying, "The smart one gives in."

That's why Lilly finally said to Sarah: "Alright, then I'll just go get the ball again."

Lilly now stood right in front of the neighbor's fence. "How am I supposed to get over there? The fence is so tall and has pointy prongs. I'm afraid I'll hurt myself if I try to climb over there," Lilly sighed, annoyed. Sarah answered, "Yes, that would be too dangerous.

You should just ring the neighbor's doorbell and ask if he can open the garden door for you and let you into his garden."

"Good idea. That would probably be the smart thing to do," Lilly accepted.

But then she felt a little queasy at the thought. There was a problem for Lilly: Her neighbor Mr. Smith. Lilly was very afraid of him.

Mr. Smith was an older man with thick white eyebrows, a gray mustache, and a bald head. He was over six feet tall. He looked pretty scary to Lilly! And he also had this deep raspy voice! Lilly had only known Mr. Smith by sight. The two had never spoken a word to each other, but Mr. Smith had talked to Lilly's parents several times.

Lilly nervously walked up to the front door of Mr. Smith's house. "How do you think Mr. Smith will react? Will he get angry and scowl at me? What happens if I start stuttering out of fear or can't get a word out at all?"

Lilly now had a thousand thoughts running through her head. Then she gathered all her courage and rang the doorbell. "Be right there," a deep male voice called out. A little later, a tall man opened the front door.

Little Lilly was now standing right in front of Mr. Smith, who was almost double her height. Lilly's heart began to pound faster and faster. "Oh, hello Lilly. What a wonderful surprise to have you ringing my doorbell today. How can I help you?" Asked Mr. Smith very kindly.

Lilly answered, stuttering, "Mr. Sm....
Smi... Smith! Hello. Sorry to bother you,
but my shuttlecock accidentally fell into
your flowerbed.

I.. I'm... I'm sorry. Can I have it back,
please?" Now that she was standing so
close to Mr. Smith, he seemed even taller
than before.  "Of course! No problem at
all. I'll unlock the garden door for you in
a minute. Then you'll have your ball back.
And just let me know the next time you
play badminton again. I'll open the garden
door for you, and you can fetch the ball
immediately if it ever flies into my garden
again," said Mr. Smith with a slight smile.
Lilly was surprised at how nice and
friendly Mr. Smith actually was. She
thanked him and carefully retrieved the

shuttlecock from the flowerbed.

"Thank you very much. Have a nice day!" Lilly said.

In a good mood and relieved, she returned to her friend Sarah with the shuttlecock. She couldn't believe the thoughts she had before and how great her fear had been earlier! As it turned out, Mr. Smith was actually a very nice and helpful man. Full of joy, Lilly and Sarah continued to play. This time, however, they kept more distance from the neighboring property. After all, they didn't want the ball to fly over again. They didn't want to disturb Mr. Smith again today.

That day, Lilly learned an important lesson. She realized that the first impression of a person could also be deceptive. Just because someone looks different or even scary doesn't mean that person can't still be very nice. If she was friendly to other people and remained polite, she didn't have to be afraid of any conversation. Lilly had shown a lot of courage, and she was mighty proud of that.

I AM GOOD
THE WAY I AM

# The bad grade

Sarah tensely sat in her seat, pushing her pencil case around on the table with a blank stare. Usually, Sarah was always in a good mood. Today, the opposite was true. "Now we'll receive our math test from last week," Sarah said to her seatmate, Linda. "Oh, that's right. Well, I thought the test was pretty easy," said Linda, who was always very good at math and obviously couldn't wait to finally find out her grade. Sarah, on the other hand, did not think the test was easy at all. She studied hard for the test, but many of the questions were just too difficult for her. Sarah feared that she would not get a good grade today.

With long strides, Sarah's teacher, Mr. Bergman, entered the classroom. He had a stack of papers in one hand and his shoulder bag in the other. Friendly as always, he greeted his students: "Good morning! I corrected your math tests yesterday. I will now go through the rows from front to back and give everyone back their test." A murmur went through the classroom. Some students began whispering frantically to each other. Others stared silently at the floor or chewed their fingernails in excitement. Sarah sat next to Linda in the second row. After a few minutes that felt like half an eternity to Sarah, Mr. Bergman arrived at Sarah and Linda's table. First, he handed Linda her test back. "Very well done," Mr.

Bergman said to Linda after placing her test on the table.

"Yay, an A!" Linda rejoiced, beaming from ear to ear. Mr. Bergman also had a slight smile on his lips. He was happy that she had once again scored an A. Now, he began to look for Sarah's work in the pile of papers. When he found it, he stopped smiling and became more serious again. Sarah began to shake with nerves.

Mr. Bergman placed Sarah's math test on the table in front of her and leaned down to her. "I actually expected a little more from you. What happened?" he asked Sarah in a low voice so the other children couldn't hear him.

Sarah looked at the red D on her math test and swallowed. "I'm not sure," Sarah said, nearly speechless.

She had an idea that she was doing worse than usual, but she really hadn't expected that grade. This was her worst grade yet. She usually received B's and C's in math. "Well, you must have had a bad day. That can happen," said Mr. Bergman. He stood up straight again and walked over to the next student. "Oh, don't worry about it. Maybe I can help you study in the future?" asked Linda, who had overheard Sarah's grade. "Yeah, maybe," Sarah answered, a little grumpy.

She wasn't in the mood to talk to her right now. Sarah lowered her head and looked at her table in a daze. She would have loved to start crying right now. She didn't want to cry in front of the other children, so she held back her tears as best she could. Fortunately, it was the last lesson, and she could go home soon. She had never felt so sad in her life.

Downhearted and with a sad face, Sarah arrived home. At lunch, her mom immediately noticed that something was off with Sarah.

"What's the matter, sweetie? Why are you so quiet today?" she inquired. Sarah just shrugged her shoulders and said, "I don't know." Then a little later, Sarah suddenly said in a shaky voice. "Remember I took that math test at school last week? Unfortunately, I got a D." Sarah was ashamed of her grade and initially thought about not telling her mom. But then she realized that there was no point in hiding anything from her mom. She would find out sooner or later anyway. Her mom was glad that her daughter finally told her what was on her mind.

"I don't think a bad grade is the end of the world, as long as you did your best. And I know you prepared diligently for the test.

Don't blame yourself for that. I'm sure you'll have many more opportunities to earn a better grade. It's not bad," her mom said.

"But it is bad," Sarah replied and continued: "You must do well in school; otherwise, you won't get a good job later on.

As you know, I want to be a veterinarian when I grow up. You need good grades for that. Besides, I'm annoyed that Linda always gets much better grades than me."

Now, all the emotions she had felt that morning at school returned. Sarah cried, and tears began to roll down her cheeks. Her mom listened to her daughter attentively and let her finish without interruption. She felt that Sarah needed that right now.

As Sarah began to calm down a bit, Mom lovingly stroked the back of her hand and said in a soft voice:

"A grade says nothing about what you can accomplish in your life. If you have a dream, the most important thing is that you believe in yourself. I will always love you very much no matter what grades you get."

Sarah wiped away her tears, took a few deep breaths, and then said, "I love you too, mom." Mom hugged Sarah and then continued talking, "Everyone can have a bad day and then not perform as well as usual. Besides, many children never earn the best grades but still go their way and later learn a profession that makes them very happy." Her mom paused for a moment to give Sarah a chance to absorb her words. "Do you actually know that you are very special just the way you are? No grade in the world will ever change that. Because grades don't determine a person's worth." Her mom gave her daughter another kiss on the cheek, and they continued eating. After finishing their meal, Mom asked, "You know what, I have an idea. Let's take a short trip to the pony farm. Are you in?"

Mom knew Sarah loved animals more than anything and they would help her quickly take her mind off things. "Yes, I'd love to. That sounds good," Sarah answered immediately.

A little later, they took the car to the nearby pony farm. Sarah fed and pet the ponies and even got to ride her favorite pony for a short time. During the excursion, Sarah was like a new person. For a moment, she forgot about the incident at school.

After dinner, Sarah went straight to bed, much earlier than usual because she had experienced so much today and was already tired. Lying in bed, she thought about what Mom had said again.
She was happy to have such a great mother. She was proud that she had been brave and talked openly with mom about her problems.

From now on, she decided never to get so sad about a bad grade again.

After all, there were much more important things in life. As Mom used to say at lunchtime, school grades don't determine a person's worth.

Satisfied, Sarah fell asleep.

# I AM
# LOVED

# The soccer game

"Sophie, Matt!" Mom called loudly from the kitchen window. "Lunch is ready! We must leave soon. Don't dilly-dally!" she continued.

Today was a beautiful, cloudless summer day. The two siblings were playing soccer together on the lawn in front of the house, as usual. Sophie had long reddish hair that she always braided into a thick braid. She loved to play on the grass with her older brother and was very skilled at soccer. Matt taught her many tricks with the ball. "All right, we'll be right there," Sophie replied and hurriedly ran into the house with her brother.

They had spaghetti with tomato sauce, one of her favorite dishes.

Now she also remembered where she was supposed to go with her mom this afternoon. Her brother had soccer practice once a week in the neighboring town. Training only stopped during vacation time. Usually, Sophie never came along. But since dad wasn't at home today to watch her, she had to go with her mom and watch her big brother practice. After all, her parents didn't want her to be home alone for that long.

"Can't I just stay here? I'll stay in my room quietly, too. I promise!" Sophie tried to convince her mother during lunch. Mom, however, answered firmly:

"No, we already discussed that yesterday, my sweetheart. It won't take long, and we can talk to each other while watching. I'm sure we won't get bored."

Sophie realized that there wasn't a point in arguing with her mom. She would much rather play with her new dolls and paint a picture for her friend Susi's birthday. They had already talked about this matter yesterday, and now she didn't see any chance to persuade her mom. She lowered her head and looked at the floor, a little disappointed and offended. She had to accept that sometimes she had to do things she didn't really want to do.

Her brother Matt tried to cheer her up, and it bubbled out of him, "You'll see, soccer with my friends is really cool. We always have a lot of fun, and I'm sure you'd like that too!" Sophie was now a little defiant and replied that she completely disagreed. It may well be that boys have fun playing soccer. She preferred just playing in the meadow alone with her brother, without keeping track of the score. She just couldn't understand why all the boys were chasing this ball and then dying to score a goal to win. She thought it was silly and would much rather continue reading her book, playing dolls, or dancing to music. "Okay," she sighed a little hesitantly, "I'll go with you then!" After lunch, they set off in the car and drove to the soccer field. It was huge. There were already a lot of boys on the green lawn.

Many people were already sitting on the stands, chatting happily with each other and watching the action. She knew a few of the boys from school and some because they were friends with her brother. Some were sprinting after the ball, while others were doing stretching exercises to warm up. One of them was her brother's best friend, and she knew him very well. His name was Tim. Three of the boys were talking excitedly with a man. He was probably their coach.

They had a lot to say to each other. Many
moms and dads squatted expectantly in
their seats, watching the kids play.
Sophie looked in all directions, but
nowhere could she see even one girl
her age. For a moment, she didn't feel
very comfortable and thought she was
completely out of place here. "Oh, mom,
I'm the only girl here!" she sighed with a
disappointed expression. "There are only
boys and adults here. See, that's why I

didn't really want to come. It's stupid!"
Sophie continued to complain. Her mom
gave her an understanding hug. Sophie
realized that her complaining wouldn't
change the situation. Now she was here
and had to deal with it.

Mom and Sophie now sat down in their
seats in the spectator stands. Mom had
taken her homemade lemonade and some
sliced fruit with her. A little snacking
passed the time more quickly. Matt came
out of the locker room and ran onto
the field, beaming with joy, to greet his
soccer friends. He loved this sport more
than anything and was also good at it.
The coach approached the assembled
team. He was a very nice, sporty-looking

gentleman with gray hair, a blue cap, and a red whistle hanging from a chain around his neck. A logo was visible on his sports jacket: Springfield Soccer Club. This was the soccer club Matt played for. The coach now stood in the middle of the field and blew loudly into the whistle. Immediately, everyone went quiet.

All players gathered right around him. "Welcome to today's training session. I hope you are all in shape. Today, we're going to have a practice match. I'm going to form two teams now, and they will play against each other," the coach explained. The boys' faces were beaming. Now they could finally show what they were capable of. Then he began to divide the boys into two groups. One team was to play in blue jerseys, the other in red. The coach brought the jerseys. He put one in each boy's hand after they were assigned to one of the two teams.

Matt and his friend Tim were on the team with the red jerseys. When the coach assigned the last boy, everyone suddenly noticed that one player was still missing from the red team. One of the boys was sick today and therefore did not show up. A murmur went through the crowd. The boys with the red jerseys knew all too well that they had no chance of winning the game if they were shorthanded. Resentment spread through the team. While the players discussed with the coach that this would be unfair, Matt had a bright idea, and he shouted into the crowd: "My sister could play. She's good with the ball. And she's here today!" Then, convinced of his suggestion, he pointed his finger in Sophie's direction. All eyes were now on her. Sophie would have liked to sink into the ground right then and there. Her face suddenly became warm, and her heart began to pound rapidly.

At first, she couldn't believe her ears when she heard her brother's suggestion.

Was she going to play soccer? As a girl? With all the boys? Gasping for air, she sought her mother's gaze. Then the coach said to Matt, "Well, that's a great idea. If your sister feels up to it, she's welcome to play on your team." The boys on Matt's team thought that was fine, too. They all stared at Sophie expectantly with wide eyes. They were curiously waiting for her decision. Sophie's heart dropped. "Do you really want me to play along? That's just for boys!" she asked mom suspiciously. Her mom whispered in her ear with her hand held out, "You can see that the boys don't mind and would love to have you on their team. But I don't want to push you into anything. I want you to make up your own mind."

Sophie thought for a moment. She was aware that she could play since she often practiced with her brother. She knew the rules of the game from TV because she had watched soccer games with Dad and Matt many times. You must kick the ball into the opponent's goal with your feet and prevent the opponent from doing the same thing at your own goal; it's not that difficult. She probably couldn't do it as well as her brother, but she didn't have to be embarrassed about that. She was just helping out. At that moment, she preferred a little movement to sitting bored in the spectators' seats. She mustered all her courage and firmly said, "Okay, I'm in!" A little giddy from her own decision, she ran onto the field and pulled the red jersey over her t-shirt. Now, it was getting serious. The coach blew the whistle for the game. In the first minutes of the game, neither team was able to score a goal.

The ball was played back and forth. It

was an even and exciting game. With full commitment, the players ran crisscross across the field. Suddenly, one of the boys from Sophie's team made a mistake. He lost the ball directly in front of his own goal. At that moment Max, a good player from the opposing team, took the chance and scored the first goal.

Oh, dear! But Sophie's team didn't let that get them down so quickly. They showed full commitment and were able to even out shortly before the end of the game. The score was now one to one. It couldn't have been more exciting. The last minutes would decide who would leave the field as the winner. Matt cheered his team on and was very proud of his sister. Sophie

proved ambition and skill and that girls are also good at soccer.
Sophie was completely focused and determined to win. Just before the end of the game, the ball landed right at her feet.

It was the very last opportunity in this game to score a goal and win. The opponents tried with all their might to take the ball from her. At that moment, Sophie saw her brother standing by at the opponent's goal. She played the ball to

Matt with a well-aimed pass. They always practiced this at home.

Matt shot at the goal hard as he could. The ball flew past the opposing goalie in a high arc and landed right in the left corner. "Goal! Goal!" cheered Sophie and her team with excitement. Matt immediately ran to his sister and hugged her. Stunned with joy, he said, "Beautiful pass, my dear little sister. I told you you'd have fun." Then a loud whistle sounded. The game was over. Sophie's team won! And she played the winning pass!

At that moment, she was incredibly happy and mighty proud of herself.

Mom also cheered from the stands and clapped with joy.

Back home, Sophie said enthusiastically: "That was really great today. What a shame there isn't a team for girls, too." "But there are also soccer teams for girls. In our club, the girls always have practice on Saturday. Maybe you'd like to go tomorrow?" replied Matt. To Sophie, that sounded like an excellent idea. Soccer had been so much fun for her today. Who knows, maybe she would play in the club like her big brother and score lots of goals one day. Maybe she would even play in big stadiums and win championships someday? Dreams are something wonderful, after all. Even though she didn't feel like it at all at first, she was now glad she went. If she hadn't overcome her fear and stayed in the stands with her mother, she would never have experienced how much fun soccer can be.

What a great day.

# I AM STRONG
# AND COURAGEOUS

# Taking the leap

"Wake up, Lisa! You have to get up now," dad called. He stood impatiently at Lisa's bedroom door and continued, "If you always dilly-dally like that, you'll be late for school." Lisa still rubbed her eyes sleepily, yawned, and then replied somewhat grumpily, "It's okay, Dad, I'll get up." She had only been woken up by her dad's call and was still tired.

She was thinking back to her dream with elves and fairies in an enchanted forest. Lisa was a cheerful girl with shoulder-length blond hair and big blue-gray eyes. Like every morning, Lisa got dressed right after getting up and brushed her teeth thoroughly. Then she neatly folded her pink pajamas with colorful stars and tidied her bed. Lisa's dad wasn't particularly strict, but tidiness was very important to him.

"Dad is right. When everything is neatly in its place, you get a much better view of things. And you can find your things more quickly without having to search for them," Lisa thought to herself.

Today, her father prepared the good cereals with nuts and mixed fruit that she loved to eat. While she was enjoying her breakfast, she suddenly remembered that today was Friday. On that day, she always had PE during the last period of school. Recently, her class started going to the swimming pool, which was just across the street from the school building.

Usually, Lisa always looked forward to PE. However, since her class started to go to the swimming pool, she didn't feel like it anymore. "What's wrong, my darling? Is something wrong?" dad asked, a little worried. Lisa's sad look into space and her hunched shoulders were always a sign to dad that something was bothering his daughter. Lisa hesitated for a moment. She then answered timidly, "We always go swimming with the whole class on Fridays now. Today we're even supposed to jump off the diving board into the pool." Almost sobbing, she continued, "Dad, I'm scared of jumping from so far up into deep water!" "Oh, Lisa!" dad replied sympathetically. "Then just explain to Mrs. Miller that you're afraid of heights, and that's why you can't jump. I'm sure she'll be able to understand."

Mrs. Miller was really a very experienced and mindful teacher. She is the teacher of class 3b and taught almost all subjects. She is very popular with her students because you can come to her when you have problems. She was even the so-called confidant teacher of the whole school. Lisa was concerned. "But what if the other kids laugh at me and call me a little chicken? And honestly... actually... actually..." she stammered on shyly," I want to try jumping. It must feel wonderful to fly in the air for a moment. Like a bird. But I'm just so incredibly afraid of it." Dad paused for a moment, thinking about how he could help Lisa. He then gently took Lisa's tender hand and spoke in a soft voice, "I'm going to tell you a secret, or rather a little trick that has always helped me overcome my fear. First, close your eyes tightly. Then you breathe in and out deeply three times, counting. Three...Two...One...and then you jump." Lisa listened in fascination, then asked, "And that really works?" Dad lowered his head, smiled, and continued, "Well, for me, that trick has always helped a lot. But for it to really work, you must believe in yourself very strongly, as firmly as I believe in you. You can do this!"

Lisa took new courage from her dad's words. She trusted him and resolved to try the trick right away today. "Ding-dong," rang the school bell for the last lesson. Now the time had come, and physical education began. Mr. Miller left the school building with the class, and they entered the swimming hall on the opposite side of the street. It was a huge hall with large glass windows.

You almost thought you were outdoors because you could see the school park from the hall. Mrs. Miller said to the assembled class, "Please put on your swimsuits and then line up in order. As I announced last week, today we are going to learn how to jump into the water from the diving board. I'm sure you'll really enjoy that!" A little anxious, Lisa walked alongside her friend Olivia to the locker rooms. Olivia was her best friend. They knew each other from preschool and lived not far from each other.

Now they went to the same class and were

seatmates. Christina was very athletic and simply loved the water. She had even been in the swim club for some time now. She was also able to jump off the tall diving boards. Liz had recently told her that with pride. "Is everything all right with you, too? You seem so different today. Are you scared?" whispered Olivia in Lisa's ear.

She had noticed, of course, that Lisa was quieter than usual and seemed tense. They were best friends and usually talked and laughed together when they saw each other. Lisa answered with her head down and her voice unsteady, "Well... I'm a little nervous already." A lump formed in her throat. She collected herself and continued speaking, "I've never jumped off the diving board into the water before, and I'm actually afraid of heights."

Lisa was glad she could talk to Olivia about anything. She was her very best friend and would never laugh at her.

"Oh, you'll be fine, Lisa. Just don't think about it too much! And besides, I'll be by your side," Olivia said.

After all the kids had changed, they lined up behind the diving board. At that moment, the diving board seemed like the highest mountain on earth to Lisa.

Her legs started shaking, and she suddenly felt like she couldn't breathe properly.

Olivia, who was standing in front of her, turned around briefly and tried to cheer her friend up: "You can do this. We'll do it together." Lisa was glad to have Olivia by her side. One by one, they jumped into the water. First, it was the boys' turn. The first one was Marc. He could hardly wait and jumped into the pool with a loud "Woohoo."

However, most of the boys jumped into the water carefully and straight as a candle while holding their noses. A few of the boys were already practiced and even made a pike. Then it was the girls' turn. Olivia was the first. She had practiced jumping into the water many hundreds of times and was excited to show everyone. It was Lisa's turn now. But she hesitated and left two other girls in front of her, who could hardly wait to jump into the cool water. It looked so easy for almost all of them.

Most of them were laughing and really having fun.

Now it was finally Lisa's turn. She was the very last one! Lisa's heart now began to thump loudly again, and her legs felt like rubber. Nevertheless, Lisa walked with slow, hesitant steps to the edge of the diving board. Her knees were shaking, and she actually wanted to turn back on the spot. In the background, she heard Olivia's familiar voice: "Come on, Olivia! Jump! It's easy."

At the same time, she remembered her dad's words again. She took a deep breath. She exhaled deeply. Three times. With each breath, her fear lessened. Lisa closed her eyes and counted in her mind. Three...

Two...One... And then she jumped. At that moment, she felt like a dolphin jumping in the air for joy and then splashing back into the sea.

It was unusually quiet as she dove into the water, but immediately she wriggled her feet and came back to the surface. What an indescribable feeling it was! She made it and was incredibly happy about it. If she hadn't dared to jump, she would never have been able to feel this joy. Lisa was very proud of herself.

She swam to the edge of the pool full of inner strength and confidence and climbed out of the water.

Olivia welcomed her with a smile: "I knew you could do it. It wasn't that hard!" Afterward, the children were allowed to play water polo and have fun in the water until the end of the sports lesson.

Back home, Lisa could hardly wait to tell her father about the experience. She was bubbling over with excitement and pride. "Dad, your trick really worked. I just jumped!" she told her dad with tears of joy in her eyes. "You did a really great job, honey. I'm so proud of you. Do you know how much I love you?" dad said to her in a soft voice, and they hugged each other.

In the evening, when they went to bed, dad lovingly kissed her goodnight, as he did every day. Then he said, "Good night, honey," and turned out the light. Lisa lay awake in bed for a while today. She couldn't fall asleep; so many thoughts were going through her head. Today she learned that she could do almost anything if she wanted to and believed in herself. Her biggest fear was jumping into the water, and she had overcome that now. Satisfied and happy with herself and the world, Lisa finally fell asleep.

I AM
LUCKY

# Imprint

**Please contact us if you have any questions, feedback or suggestions:**
info@pisionary.com

The author is represented by: Pisionary Publishing Ltd
Evagora Laniti, O3 Adonis Village, Aphrodite Hills, Kouklia 8509
Year of publication: 2022
Responsible for printing: Amazon

**Dear Girl: You are Amazing**
Emily Green
ISBN: 9798843910280
2nd edition 2022
© 2022 Emily Green, pisionary